P9-CBR-637

J A SERIES
Roy, Ron
The deadly dungeon

091509

D is for Danger...

Suddenly a scream burst from the castle behind them.

Dink nearly dropped his end of the picnic basket. The skin on his arms erupted into a thousand goose bumps.

The kids looked at each other, wide-eyed.

Wallis glanced back and grinned. "Dink, Josh, Ruth Rose, allow me to introduce...the ghost of Emory Scott!"

The A to Z Mysteries™ series!

The Absent Author
The Bald Bandit
The Canary Caper
The Deadly Dungeon

For Emily and Zach
–R.R.

To Emily, for being a great Ruth Rose
–J.S.G.

Text copyright © 1998 by Ron Roy.
Illustrations copyright © 1998 by John Steven Gurney.
All rights reserved under International and Pan-American Copyright Conventions.
Published in the United States by Random House, Inc., New York, and simultaneously in Canada by Random House of Canada Limited, Toronto.

http://www.randomhouse.com/

Library of Congress Cataloging-in-Publication Data
Roy, Ron. The deadly dungeon / by Ron Roy ; illustrated by John Gurney.
   p.   cm. — (A to Z mysteries) "A Stepping Stone book."
SUMMARY: While visiting Wallis's castle, Dink and his friends investigate strange noises that lead them to a dangerous secret.
ISBN 0-679-88755-5 (pbk.) — ISBN 0-679-98755-X (lib. bdg.)
[1. Castles — Fiction.   2. Mystery and detective stories.]   I. Gurney, John, ill.   II. Title.
III. Series: Roy, Ron. A to Z mysteries.
PZ7.R8139De 1998 [Fic]—dc21 97-27566

Printed in the United States of America   10 9 8 7

A to Z Mysteries™

The Deadly Dungeon

by Ron Roy

illustrated by
John Steven Gurney

A STEPPING STONE BOOK™

Random House 🏠 New York

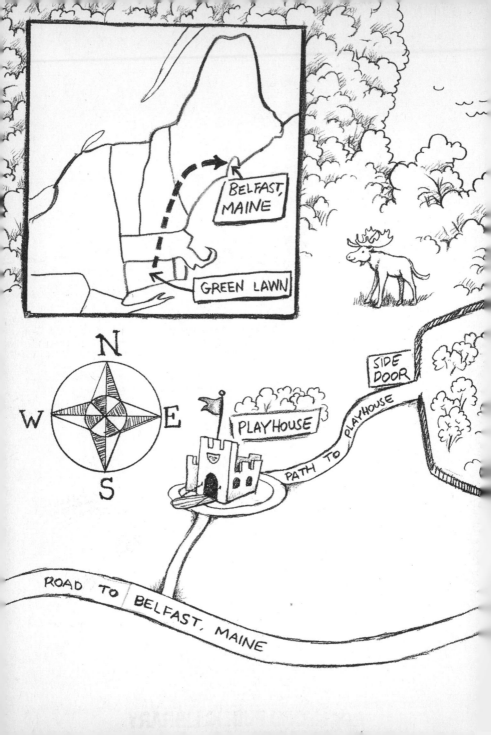

BELFAST, MAINE

GREEN LAWN

N
W E
S

PLAYHOUSE

SIDE DOOR

PATH TO PLAYHOUSE

ROAD TO BELFAST, MAINE

Welcome to **A to Z Mysteries**
on Location
at Moose Manor

ATLANTIC
OCEAN

MOAT
GARDEN

CASTLE

STEPS
TO
BEACH

MOAT

FRONT
DOOR

DRAWBRIDGE

PICNIC
BEACH

Chapter 1

Dink squirmed in his seat. He, Josh, and Ruth Rose had been riding the bus since seven that morning.

They were on their way to Maine to visit their friend Wallis Wallace, a famous mystery writer. The three of them had met her when she came to Green Lawn. Dink smiled when he remembered how they had rescued Wallis from a "kidnapper."

Dink glanced over at Josh, asleep in his seat. His sketch pad was open on his lap.

Behind Josh, Ruth Rose was looking at a map. She liked to dress in one color. Today it was green, from her T-shirt to her high-tops.

Dink moved into the seat next to Ruth Rose. "Where are we?" he asked.

"Almost there." She pointed to Belfast, Maine, on her map. "We just passed a Welcome to Belfast sign."

Dink nodded. That was where Wallis was picking them up.

Ruth Rose tucked her map into her pack. "I'm so excited!" she said. "Do you think her castle has a moat and a dungeon?"

"I just hope it has food," Dink said. "I'm starving!"

Josh's head popped up in front of them. "Me too! Are we there yet?"

Just then the bus driver called out, "Belfast!"

"All right!" Josh said, leaping into the aisle.

The bus stopped in front of a small gray-shingled building. Through the window, Dink could see the water.

"Do you see Wallis?" Ruth Rose asked.

Dink grabbed his pack. "No, but let's get off. I think I'm allergic to buses!"

The kids headed for the front. They followed an elderly couple down the steps.

They were squinting into the blinding sunlight when they heard someone say, "Hi, kids!" A tall man with curly blond hair was walking toward them. His face was tanned and smiling.

"I remember you. You're Wallis's brother!" Ruth Rose said.

"Call me Walker, okay?" said the

man. "Wallis is buying groceries, so she asked me to get you."

Walker Wallace picked up Dink's pack. It clunked heavily against his leg.

"What's in here, your rock collection?" he asked.

Dink grinned. "Books. My mom said it rains a lot in Maine, so I came prepared."

Walker laughed. "We've planned perfect weather for you guys. Sun every day! Come on, that's my Jeep over there."

Walker's dusty brown Jeep had no top. The leather seats were worn and split in places.

He swept a pair of boots and a tool belt onto the floor, making room in the backseat. "Pile in!"

The boys climbed into the back. Ruth Rose sat next to Walker. "How far is the castle?" she asked.

"Not far." Walker pointed. "About a mile past those trees."

He drove up the coast. "You guys hungry? Sis is buying everything in the store for you."

"I'm *always* hungry," Josh said, leaning back and crossing his legs. He took a deep breath of the ocean air. "What a smell!"

"I'll say," Dink said. "Get your smelly foot out of my face!"

"It's not smelly," Josh said, wiggling his sneaker under Dink's nose.

"What's this?" Dink plucked a bright green feather off the sole of Josh's sneaker.

Josh shrugged. "I must've picked it up on the bus."

Dink slipped the feather into his pocket.

"There's Moose Manor!" Walker called. He pointed through the trees.

Dink stared at the tall castle. It was built of huge gray stones. Its small dark windows looked like watching eyes. An iron fence surrounded the building.

"Cool," Dink said softly.

"Look, guys, a moat!" Ruth Rose said.

"And a drawbridge!" cried Josh.

Walker pulled up in front of the gate. The kids hopped out with their packs.

"I have to get back to my boat," Walker said. "Sis should be here soon. Have fun!" He waved and sped back through the trees.

Up close, the castle towered over the kids. The battlements on top reminded Dink of giant's teeth.

Josh pushed the gate, and it creaked open. They peered down into the moat. Ruth Rose let out a laugh. "Look, guys!"

The bottom of the empty moat was planted with flowers!

"Hey, guys!" Josh called. "Check this out!" He had crossed the drawbridge and was standing in front of an enormous wooden door. He tugged on the handle, but the door wouldn't budge. "How the heck does Wallis get in?"

Just then Dink heard a car. A red Volkswagen convertible zoomed up to the gate. The horn tooted, and a hand waved wildly.

"It's Wallis!" shouted Dink.

Chapter 2

"Welcome!" Wallis yelled.

She looked the same as Dink remembered: happy smile, curly brown hair, mischievous eyes.

"What do you think of Moose Manor?" she asked. "Isn't it fun?"

"I love it!" said Ruth Rose.

"It's awesome!" Josh said.

Wallis laughed. "It is something, isn't it? Help me with these groceries, and I'll take you on the grand tour!"

The entrance to the castle turned out to be a regular-sized door around the corner. Wallis and the kids carried bags of groceries into a large room. Dink saw a washer and dryer, wooden pegs for hats and coats, and a pile of sneakers and boots.

"This is my mud room," Wallis said. "The kitchen is through here." She shoved open another door with her hip.

Dink had to tip his head back to see the high ceiling. The usual kitchen stuff was there, with a long wooden table in the middle. A black chandelier hung over the table.

"This place is humongous!" Dink said.

"That's why I love it," Wallis said. "Let's put the food away and I'll show you around."

The kids quickly emptied the bags while Wallis put the milk and ice cream into the refrigerator.

"Okay, the tour begins in the royal

living room," Wallis said. "Follow me!" She led them into the biggest living room Dink had ever seen.

The first thing Dink noticed was the chandelier hanging right over his head. It was as big as Wallis's car!

A marble fireplace took up almost one whole wall. The mantel was dark wood, carved with all kinds of animals.

"This place is amazing!" Dink said.

"Geez," Josh breathed, peering into the fireplace. "You could burn a whole tree in here!"

Wallis flopped onto a pile of floor cushions. "Some winter days I wish I could," she said. "It gets mighty cold up on this cliff."

"How old is this place?" Ruth Rose asked, peering up at the tall stone walls.

"Pretty old," Wallis said. "It was built in the 1930s by a movie star named Emory Scott."

"Awesome!" Josh said.

"What happened to him?" Dink asked.

"Well..." Wallis raised her eyebrows and lowered her voice. "According to the town gossip, he died suddenly. Right here in the castle. In fact, sometimes I think I hear his ghost!"

The kids stared with open mouths.

Then Dink laughed. "Come on, you're just kidding, right?"

"Why? Don't you believe in ghosts?" Wallis asked with a grin.

"No way!" they all yelled.

"Well..." Wallis stood up. "Maybe Emory will introduce himself when he's ready. In the meantime, why don't I show you your rooms?"

The kids grabbed their packs and followed Wallis up a wide stone staircase to the second floor. At the top of the stairs was a dim hallway with several doors.

Wallis pointed to one. "That's my room. Ruth Rose, yours is there, and I've put you boys together, right across the hall."

Wallis tapped on a narrow door at the end of the hall. "This one leads up to the roof."

Dink opened the door to their bedroom. Like the rooms downstairs, the ceiling was high. A blue carpet covered the stone floor. The twin beds had bright red covers.

Dink went to the window and looked outside. All he could see were pine trees. "Where's the ocean?" he asked.

"On the other side," Wallis said. "Why don't you settle in, then come down for lunch?"

Ruth Rose went to her room. Dink and Josh dumped their packs on their beds.

"This place is so cool," Josh said, wandering into their bathroom.

Dink stacked his books on the table next to his bed. He pawed through his clothes, then changed into shorts and a T-shirt.

"Dink, come in here!" Josh called.

Dink wandered into the bathroom.

"Listen," Josh said. He had his ear against one of the bathroom walls.

"What're you doing?" asked Dink.

Josh made a shushing sound. "I thought I heard something!"

"What's going on?" Ruth Rose said as she came into the room.

"Josh thought he heard something behind the wall," Dink said.

Ruth Rose grinned. "It must be the ghost of Emory Scott. He's just waiting for you two to fall asleep tonight!"

Just then they heard Wallis's voice. "Come and get it!" she called. They raced down to the kitchen.

Wallis was packing a basket. "It's such a great day, I thought we'd have a picnic on the beach," she said.

"Cool!" Josh said. "Can we go fishing there sometime?"

Wallis nodded. "Ask Walker if you can borrow some gear. In fact, he's taking you lobstering tomorrow."

"Awesome!" Josh yelled.

Wallis smiled. "You won't think so at four-thirty tomorrow morning."

Dink and Josh each grabbed one end of the picnic basket. Wallis handed Ruth Rose a blanket, then led them to the back of the castle and through another gate.

"Great view, isn't it?" Wallis said. "The first time I saw this place, I knew I had to do my writing here."

Dink took a deep breath of the sea air. Small boats made colorful dots against the blue ocean. "It's really nice," he said.

Josh peered nervously over the cliff. "How do we get down?"

Wallis laughed. "See there? I had steps built. But poor Emory Scott! You remember that marble fireplace and that massive chandelier? Every piece came from Europe by boat. Goodness knows how he got them up this cliff!"

Suddenly a scream burst from the castle behind them.

Dink nearly dropped his end of the picnic basket. The skin on his arms erupted into a thousand goose bumps.

Wallis glanced back and grinned. "Dink, Josh, Ruth Rose, allow me to introduce...the ghost of Emory Scott!"

Chapter 3

The kids stared at Wallis in silence.

She winked at them. "Don't worry, that's just his way of saying hello. Shall we go down?"

The kids glanced at each other, then followed Wallis down the wooden stairs. At the bottom they found a small, sandy beach.

Dink and Josh set the basket in the shade of some boulders while Wallis and Ruth Rose spread the blanket.

"Look! A cave!" Josh said, pointing at a tunnel at the bottom of the cliff. The sea snaked into the dark hole, making a narrow river.

"How far does it go in?" Josh asked, peering into the black space.

"I don't know," Wallis said. "Walker

told me that it's full of bats."

They picnicked on chicken sand-wiches, apples, chocolate chip cookies, and cold lemonade. Wallis pointed down the shoreline. "Walker's house is beyond those trees."

"Where is he?" asked Dink.

"Out on his boat," Wallis said, wav-ing a cookie at the ocean. "His lobster pots are scattered over about a half mile of very deep water."

"How does he find them?" Josh asked.

Wallis wiped her fingers on a paper napkin. "Well, he has a good compass aboard *Lady Luck*—that's his boat—and he knows the water."

After their picnic, Wallis put every-thing back into the basket. "Ready for a walk?"

They hiked along the rocky beach. Ruth Rose poked into tide pools and picked up shells. Josh hung his sneakers around his neck and waded along the shore.

"Better watch out for lobsters," Dink teased. "They like smelly toes."

Josh grinned and splashed Dink.

Rounding a curve in the shoreline, Wallis pointed. "There's Walker's place."

It was a gray cottage with a red roof, surrounded by dune grass and sand.

Just then they heard a shout. Dink looked around and saw someone waving from the end of a dock.

Wallis waved back. "Kids, come and meet our friend Ripley Pearce."

They walked out on the dock toward a long green boat tied at the end. The boat's brass and wood trim gleamed in the sunlight.

A man stood next to the boat, holding a dripping sponge. He had dark slicked-back hair and blue eyes.

"Hi, Rip," Wallis said. "Meet Dink Duncan, Josh Pinto, and Ruth Rose Hathaway."

The man smiled and stuck out a hand. He had dazzling white teeth and a deep tan. "You're fans of this lady's books, right?"

"I've got all of them!" Dink announced.

"I met these three in Connecticut," Wallis explained. "They're spending a week up at the castle. Why don't you come for supper with us tonight?"

"I like your boat," Ruth Rose said. "It's so shiny and clean!"

Rip flashed her a grin. "Thank you very much, little lady. I'll see you tonight at dinner."

Then he looked at Josh. "Want to untie me?" he asked, pointing to a rope tied to the end of the dock.

Josh untied the rope and handed it to Rip.

"Nice meeting you kids," he said, stepping aboard his boat. He started the engine, and the boat pulled smoothly away from the dock.

Dink watched the boat cut through the water. "Maybe I won't be a writer when I grow up. Maybe I'll get a lobster boat."

Wallis grinned at Dink. "Better stick to writing, Dink. Lobsters are getting scarce in Maine."

"I can't wait to go out on Walker's boat," Ruth Rose said.

"My brother's boat is nothing like Rip's," Wallis said. She shook her head. "I don't know how Rip keeps his so clean. Walker's boat looks and smells like a lobster boat."

They walked back toward their picnic spot. Josh kicked water on Ruth

Rose, and she chased him down the beach, yelling all the way.

Dink walked quietly along with Wallis. Overhead, a sea gull cried out.

Dink looked up at Wallis. "Do you really think that scream we heard was the ghost of Emory Scott?"

Wallis laughed. "All I know is I've been hearing those screams since I moved in. The first time, I searched the castle. But I never found a thing."

Dink shivered. "Do you hear the noises a lot?" he asked.

Wallis shrugged. "Sometimes weeks go by and there's not a peep. Then I'll hear them for a few days in a row."

Wallis smiled down at Dink. "To tell you the truth, Dink, this is one mystery that's got me stumped. If those screams aren't the ghost of Emory Scott, I don't know what they are!"

Chapter 4

At the top of the cliff, Wallis took the picnic things. "I need to spend some time working on my new book," she said. "Why don't you guys go exploring? Emory Scott built a playhouse for his kids in those trees. You might want to check it out."

She opened the side door. "Oh, I almost forgot," she said with twinkling eyes. "Some people think his ghost hangs around there, looking for his children. So keep your eyes open!" With that, she went inside.

The kids found a path through the trees. As they walked, Dink told Josh and Ruth Rose what Wallis had said on the beach.

"So it *is* a ghost!" Josh said. "Creepy!"

"No way," Ruth Rose said. "I don't believe in ghosts. It must be an animal trapped somewhere in the castle."

"I don't know," Dink said. "Wallis told me she searched the whole place."

"Besides," said Josh, "what kind of animal makes a spooky scream like that?"

Just then the kids reached the playhouse. The outside of the small wooden building had been painted to look like Wallis's castle. A kid-sized drawbridge crossed a shallow moat to the front door.

"Excellent," said Josh.

"Let's go inside!" Ruth Rose cried, running to the door. She tugged on the handle, and the door opened with a soft whoosh.

Ruth Rose curtsied. "Enter, my loyal knights!"

"His Highness King Dink goes first," Dink said, nudging ahead of Josh.

They crowded into the room. Everything was covered with a layer of dust. Dim light shone through two small windows covered with cobwebs.

Josh rubbed his arms. "Boy, this place is cold," he said.

"Looks like no one's been in here for years," Ruth Rose said.

A round table and two little chairs stood in the middle of the room on a dusty, worn rug. A shelf held a miniature set of blue dishes. Under the shelf, a lonely-looking teddy bear sat on an old sofa.

"This place creeps me out," Josh said.

"Look," Dink said. "Footprints on the rug." He stepped into one of them. "Whoever made these sure has big feet!"

"Do ghosts leave footprints?" Josh asked.

"Maybe it's Walker," Ruth Rose suggested. "They're too big to be Wallis's."

"But why would Walker come here?" Dink wondered out loud.

"Can we go?" Josh pleaded. "I just saw a monster spider, and he was looking back at me!"

"Okay, but let's come back," Ruth Rose said. "I want to clean this place. It's sad to see it all dusty like this."

Ruth Rose pulled the door shut behind them. As they crossed the drawbridge, Dink noticed something in the moat. He jumped down and picked up a bright green feather.

"Hey, guys, look! It's like the one that was stuck to Josh's sneaker."

Ruth Rose held the feather up to the sun. "What's it from?"

Josh examined the feather. "The only bird I know with this kind of feather is a parrot," he said. "But parrots don't live in Maine."

Dink took the feather back from

Josh, then put it in his pocket.

"Okay, we've explored the play-house," Josh said. "Now you guys have to do what I want."

Dink grinned at his friend. "You mean eat?"

"No. I want to check out that cave down on the beach."

"Wait a minute," Dink said. "You were creeped out by the playhouse, but you want to explore the cave?"

"Caves are cool," Josh said. "Come on, you guys."

The kids headed past the castle, through the gate, and down the cliff. They stood looking at the small river flowing out of the cave. "I wonder how deep it is," Dink said.

"There's one way to find out," Josh said. He stepped in the water and began wading into the cave. The water reached just above his ankles.

"Come on, you guys!" he called over his shoulder.

Dink and Ruth Rose followed him. The cave grew darker, until the sunlight disappeared. The air was cold and damp, and the black walls felt slimy.

"Josh, this water is freezing," Ruth Rose said. Her voice sounded hollow. "I hate it in here! Can we go back?"

"The water's getting deeper, too," Dink said. "And I can't even see you guys!"

"Shh!" Josh said. "I heard something!"

"Josh, don't try to scare us!" Ruth Rose said. "I'm already—"

Suddenly a scream echoed through the cave.

"RUN!" Ruth Rose yelled.

Over their heads, hundreds of black bats streaked for daylight.

Chapter 5

The kids didn't stop running till they were at the top of the cliff. Dink threw himself on the ground, trying to catch his breath.

"What was that?" Ruth Rose asked, pulling off her sopping sneakers. "My heart nearly stopped!"

"It was the ghost!" Josh said. "I bet that cave leads to a secret dungeon under the castle. Maybe that's where Emory Scott died!"

Ruth Rose burst out laughing. Josh ignored her. "There must be a secret

door leading to the dungeon somewhere. And I'm going to find it!"

"Maybe you are," Dink said. "But
I'm gonna take a shower and change."

"Me too," Ruth Rose said. "I smell
like a fish!"

When they got back to the castle,
Walker's Jeep was parked out front.
The kids cleaned up, then hurried
down to the kitchen. Wallis, Walker,
and Rip were sitting at the long table,
husking ears of corn.

"Hi, kids," Walker said. "How was
your first day at Moose Manor?"

"It was great," Josh said, shooting
Dink a look. "We explored the play-

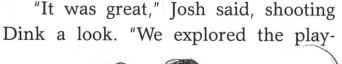

house and found some neat stuff on the beach."

Dink figured Josh wanted to keep his "secret dungeon" idea to himself.

"Well, I have lobsters to cook," Wallis said. "I hope everyone's hungry!"

After supper, the grownups decided to play Scrabble.

"You kids can join us," Wallis said. "Or you can choose another board game from the hall closet. Help yourself."

"Um...I think I'll go upstairs and read," Josh said. He motioned for Dink and Ruth Rose to follow him. They met upstairs in the hall between the bedrooms. "Let's search up here while they're playing Scrabble," he said.

"What exactly are we looking for?" Dink asked.

"A secret door or passageway," Josh

said, rapping his knuckle lightly on a wall.

"Josh, don't you think Wallis would've told us about a secret door?" Ruth Rose said.

"Maybe she doesn't know about it," Josh said.

"I guess we should look around," Dink agreed. *"Something* is making those weird noises."

"Let's start on the roof," Ruth Rose said.

They walked down the hall, and Josh pushed open the narrow door.

At the top of the stairs, they opened another door. A cool breeze blew in their faces as they stepped onto the flat roof.

"Wow! You can see everything!" said Josh. "It would be neat to fly a kite up here!"

Dink stood between two granite

battlements that were taller than he was. He felt like a king looking over his land.

"There's nothing up here," Josh said.

"Okay," Dink said. "Let's look downstairs."

The kids tromped back down to the hall.

Ruth Rose walked into her room while Dink and Josh searched theirs. Dink started with the closet, but found only dust and an old tennis racket.

He used the racket to poke behind the window curtains. A few spiders darted away, but nothing else.

Suddenly Josh screamed from the bathroom. "Dink, it's got me! Help!"

Dink charged into the bathroom, holding the tennis racket like a club. He looked around wildly, but the room was empty.

"Josh? Where are you?"

The shower curtain flew open. Josh stood there, grinning. "Boo!"

Dink shook his head. "You're so lame, Josh. It would serve you right if some ghost did get you!"

Josh climbed out of the tub. "Thought you didn't believe in ghosts, Dinkus!"

Dink just shook his head again. He crossed the hall and knocked on Ruth Rose's door. "Find anything?" he asked.

She shook her head. "Nope."

She and Dink searched the long hall. They looked behind the radiators and inside plant pots and one tall umbrella stand.

Josh tapped on the walls, listening for hollow sounds. Finally they gave up, sweaty and dusty.

"I don't know where else to search," Dink said.

"We didn't check out the downstairs rooms," Josh said.

"We'll have to wait till tomorrow," Ruth Rose said, yawning. "I'm going to bed. And I hope I don't dream about ghosts, thanks to Josh Pinto!"

Josh grinned. "I read somewhere that ghosts eat girls with curls."

"Just let one try!" she said, then slammed her door.

Dink and Josh climbed into bed. A few minutes later they were both asleep.

Dink woke suddenly, his heart thumping. He looked at the clock. It was midnight!

Dink climbed out of bed and tiptoed to the window. He saw black trees against a blacker sky.

Then he saw it—a ghostly light near the playhouse!

Chapter 6

Dink gulped and felt goose bumps climbing his legs. Could it be Emory Scott's ghost?

The light winked a few more times, then disappeared.

Dink shivered, rubbing his eyes. When the light didn't return, he crawled back into bed.

He yawned and closed his eyes, deciding that he had seen a firefly.

But just before falling off to sleep, Dink opened his eyes again. He had seen only one light moving out there in the darkness.

Why would there be only one firefly in the woods? He thought about that until he fell asleep.

Dink dreamed that he was in the cave again. It was pitch dark. Up ahead, he heard a hideous scream. But this time, the scream didn't stop, it just got louder. Suddenly bats were flying in his face. But these bats had feathers—bright green feathers!

Dink bolted upright in his bed. The blankets were twisted around his legs and the alarm clock was buzzing.

I'm not in a cave, Dink realized. I'm still in the castle. Relieved, he shut off the alarm.

"Josh, wake up," he said.

Josh opened an eye. "Why?"

Dink climbed out of bed. "Walker's taking us lobstering, remember?" He turned on the light and yanked Josh's covers off.

"Come on, let's go catch a lobster!"

Josh groaned, but he climbed out of bed. "I hate lobsters."

Dink laughed. "You ate one last night." He pulled on yesterday's jeans and a warm sweatshirt over his T-shirt. "I'm going downstairs. Don't go back to bed!"

Dink crossed the hall and tapped on Ruth Rose's door. She was up and dressed in yellow from top to bottom.

"Did you see anything strange last night?" Dink asked.

Ruth Rose was pulling a brush through her hair. She shook her head.

"Well, I did! I'll tell you about it downstairs."

There was a light on in the kitchen. Dink saw juice glasses, cereal bowls, and some muffins on the table. He was munching when Ruth Rose and Josh came in.

"Guys, I think someone was creeping around outside last night," Dink said. He told them about the light he'd seen in the woods.

Josh grabbed a muffin and bit off half.

"Told you," he said, trying to grin and chew at the same time. "It was Emory's ghost!"

"Very funny, Josh," Ruth Rose said.

Just then there was a thump in the mud room and the kitchen door crashed open. Josh nearly fell out of his chair.

Walker came in wearing tall rubber boots and a yellow slicker. "Ready to go?" he asked.

Dink laughed in relief. "Josh thought you were a ghost," he said.

"Did not," Josh muttered.

They walked outside and climbed into Walker's Jeep. The sky was pitch black. Dink peered into the woods, half expecting to see the strange light again.

A few minutes later Walker turned into his driveway. They got out and walked behind the house to the dock. Their feet made hollow noises on the wooden boards.

"Watch your step out here," Walker said, aiming a flashlight at Dink's feet.

Dink breathed in the salty night air. A few stars made pinpoints of light above the boat. Somewhere, he heard a night bird call.

"Ready to come aboard?" Walker asked.

Dink, Josh, and Ruth Rose followed Walker onto the dark boat.

Chapter 7

"Better slip one of those on," Walker said when they were aboard. He pointed at orange life jackets hanging on a row of pegs.

The kids climbed into the bulky vests and sat on benches. Walker started the motor, and the small boat moved away from the dock.

"It'll be about an hour before we get to my pots," Walker hollered over the roar of the engine. "Get comfortable!"

Ruth Rose and Josh curled up on the benches, but Dink sat up. He didn't want to miss a thing. He could smell the lobster bait. Waves slapped against the hull as they chugged through the black water.

Dink watched the glow of morning color the horizon pale yellow. It made him remember the light he'd seen last night. Did the light have anything to do with the strange noises or the two green feathers?

The boat's gentle rocking made Dink feel sleepy. He closed his eyes. Then Walker was shaking him. Dink sat up and squinted into sunlight.

The waves rocked the boat back and forth. When Dink stood, he nearly lost his balance. "Where are we?" he asked.

"About five miles out," Walker said. "Wake up Ruth Rose and Josh, and we'll eat."

They sat in a patch of sunlight. Breakfast was peanut butter sandwiches and hot, milky cocoa from Walker's thermos.

Dink saw other boats in the distance. "Are those all lobster boats?"

Walker nodded. "Most of them are. A few fishing boats are out, too."

Josh looked over the side. "How do you catch the lobsters?" he asked.

Walker pointed to a machine. "That winch brings them up. I'll show you how it works."

Walker picked up a long pole with a hook on one end. He used it to grab the rope attached to a marker buoy. He snagged the rope onto the winch, pushed a button, and wet rope began whistling up out of the water. Fast!

A few seconds later a lobster pot surfaced on the other end of the rope. Wearing a rubber apron and gloves, Walker dragged it into the boat.

The wooden trap was covered with

seaweed. A few small crabs scampered out onto the deck. "Let's see what we've got," Walker said, dropping the crabs back into the sea.

Walker opened the pot's small door and reached in a gloved hand. He pulled out a wet, dark green lobster. The lobster waved its claws angrily.

"Those claws can break a finger," Walker warned. He snapped two thick rubber bands onto the lobster's front claws. Then he dropped the lobster into a tank of sea water.

"Josh, get the bait, will you?"

Josh dragged the heavy pail over. Walker pulled out a huge fish head.

"Oh, phew!" Josh said. "That's gross!"

"The lobsters don't mind," Walker said, dropping the fish head into the lobster pot. He fastened the door and shoved the trap back into the water.

"That's pretty much how it's done," Walker said, slapping water off his gloves.

"Can we pull another one?" Dink asked.

"Sure, and you guys can help. Grab some gloves out of that locker."

Ruth Rose brought out three pairs of

thick rubber gloves. Walker winched up another pot and held a wiggling lobster out to Josh.

"Hold him by the back so he can't reach you with his claws."

Josh held the lobster with both gloved hands. Ruth Rose and Dink snapped rubber bands onto the claws.

"Who wants to put bait in the pot?" Walker asked, grinning.

Dink volunteered while Josh faked gagging noises. Dink stuck his hand into the bait bucket, then dropped a bloody fish head into the lobster pot.

The morning grew warm, so the kids stripped off their sweatshirts. The ocean was calm. Sea gulls soared overhead, watching for scraps.

"Look, there's Rip," Walker said.

Rip pulled his boat up next to *Lady Luck*. When the boats were side by side, Rip tossed a line to Dink.

"How's it going?" Rip asked. He was wearing clean jeans and a T-shirt. He held a coffee mug in one hand.

"We got a few," Walker said. "My crew here was a big help."

"Are you going lobstering?" Josh asked.

Rip shook his head and flashed a grin. "Not today, kiddo. Just came out to check my buoys. Toss me the line, okay?"

Dink tossed his end of the rope toward the other boat. Rip caught it in his free hand. "Have a good day!" he yelled as he pulled away.

"Anyone want more cocoa?" Walker asked.

"I do," Josh said.

Dink turned around and saw something on *Lady Luck*'s deck.

It was a bright green feather.

Chapter 8

Dink snatched up the feather. Ruth Rose raised her eyebrows. Dink shrugged and stuck the feather in his pocket.

"Ready to head in?" Walker asked. "I promised Sis I'd get you back before lunch."

He started up the engine, and they chugged toward land.

Back at Walker's dock, the kids helped him hose fish goo and seaweed off the deck of his boat. Then he drove them to the castle.

"Sis's car is gone," Walker said. "She must be out doing errands. Will you kids be okay for a while?"

"I'm a little hungry," Josh said, grinning.

"Here, finish this." Walker handed Josh the bread, peanut butter, and knife. He waved and drove away.

"Where should we eat?" Josh asked.

"How about the playhouse?" Ruth Rose said. "I can wash those little dishes." She found a watering can next to the mud room door and filled it from the spigot.

On the way to the playhouse, Dink pulled the feathers out of his pocket. He told Josh how he'd found the third one on Walker's boat.

The kids studied the feathers, holding them up to the sunlight. "They're exactly alike," Josh said.

"Another parrot feather?" Ruth Rose

asked. "Where could they be coming from?"

Josh grinned. "From a parrot?"

"Very funny, Joshua!"

Dink suddenly remembered his dream. Screaming bats with green feathers...

Ruth Rose opened the playhouse door and they walked in.

"It's too cold in here," Josh said. "Why don't we eat out in the sun?"

Dink helped Josh carry the table out.

Ruth Rose brought out the dishes and set them in the grass.

"The rug looks pretty dusty," Dink said. "We should drag it outside and sweep it."

Josh was spreading peanut butter on bread at the table. "Can we eat first, then work? My stomach is talking to me."

On his knees, Dink began rolling up the rug. "Your stomach is—hey, guys, look!"

"Not another green feather, I hope," Josh muttered. He strolled over to see.

Dink pointed to a trapdoor in the floor.

"Yes!" Josh yelled. "I told you! The secret door to the secret dungeon!"

Ruth Rose ran over. "Let's open it!" she said.

The handle had a spring lock. Ruth Rose squeezed the spring, and the lock popped open. With all three of them pulling, they were able to raise the trapdoor. They heard a creepy whoosh, then cold, damp air escaped.

"Yuck, what a smell!" Josh said.

The kids stared into the musty-smelling hole. Stone steps led down to darkness. Even in the dim light, they saw footprints on the steps.

"Just like the prints we saw on the rug," Dink said.

They all jumped back as a hollow scream echoed out of the dark hole.

Chapter 9

"Something's down there!" Ruth Rose whispered.

Josh's eyes were huge. "Not some-*thing*," he whispered. "Some*one*. It's the ghost of Emory Scott!"

Dink put his hand in his pocket and felt the three green parrot feathers.

Taking a deep breath, he put a foot on the top step. "I'm going down," he said.

Dink walked down the steps, feeling along the cold stone walls. He tried not to think about slimy things that hung out in damp tunnels.

Then his hand touched something square and hard. A light switch! He flipped it up, and the space was suddenly flooded with light.

"It's a long tunnel!" he yelled.

Ruth Rose hurried down the steps. She turned to Josh. "Coming?"

"All right," Josh sighed. "But if anything touches me, I'm out of here!"

The tunnel was cold and narrow. They walked along the dirt floor. Small, cobweb-covered light bulbs hung from the ceiling. The air smelled rotten.

The tunnel went straight for a while, then turned a corner.

"Listen," Ruth Rose said. "I hear water."

"I hate this," Josh said. "I really do."

Dink turned the corner and found himself standing in water. Something let out a screech, and Dink froze.

Josh grabbed Dink around the neck.

"What the heck was that?" he squeaked.

"Josh, you're strangling me!" Dink croaked.

"Sorry," Josh said.

"Where are we?" Ruth Rose asked.

They were standing at the entrance to a cave. The rock walls oozed, and the floor was under water. Off to the left, another tunnel continued out of sight.

"I think I know where we are," Dink whispered.

"Me too," Josh said. "We're in the dungeon. I'd better not see any skeletons!"

"I think if we'd kept going through the cave yesterday," Dink continued, "we'd have ended up here."

"It's one long tunnel," Ruth Rose said. "From the playhouse to the ocean!"

Then something behind them made a loud squawk.

Josh jumped, nearly knocking Dink over.

"Look, guys," Ruth Rose said. "Over there!" She pointed to a dark mound up against one wall.

Dink walked over, splashing through the cold water.

"It's a tarp," he said.

Holding his breath, Dink grabbed one corner and yanked it away. Under the tarp were two cages, one on top of the other. Each cage held four large green parrots.

The birds panicked, beating their wings against the cage bars. Their screams echoed again and again off the cave walls.

"So much for the ghost of Emory Scott," Ruth Rose said.

Josh laughed. "Good! I don't know what I'd have done if I'd bumped into him!"

Dink pulled the feathers from his pocket. He held them next to one of the parrots.

"They're the same," he said.

"What the heck *is* this place?" Ruth Rose asked. "Who'd hide parrots in a cave?"

"I don't know," Dink said.

"Guys!" Ruth Rose said. She was looking down. "The tide must be coming in. The water is getting deeper!"

Dink and Josh looked down. The water was up to their ankles!

"The parrots!" Josh said.

The bottom cage was getting wet. The parrots shrieked at the rising water.

"Let's get them outside!" Dink said, grabbing the top cage. He lugged it into the dry tunnel.

Josh and Ruth Rose took the other cage. They hurried back along the tunnel with the parrots squawking in fear.

Dink stopped at the bottom of the stone steps and looked up. "Uh-oh."

"What?" Ruth Rose gasped.

"I thought we left the trapdoor open," Dink said.

"We did," Josh said.

"Well, it's closed now." Dink set his cage on the floor. He walked up the steps and pushed on the door. It didn't budge.

Josh climbed the steps, and they both shoved against the door.

"It's no use," Dink said. "The door must have fallen, and the lock snapped shut."

"What can we do?" Ruth Rose asked. "If the tide floods this tunnel..."

Dink walked back down the steps. "There's another way out. But we'll have to swim."

Chapter 10

"Where?" Ruth Rose asked.

"We can go back to the cave and swim out through the tunnel," Dink explained.

"But there are bats in there!"

"It's our only way out," Josh said.

The kids lugged the two cages back through the tunnel. The parrots screeched and beat their wings.

In the cave, the water was almost up to their knees, and rising.

"We better get out of here fast," Josh said.

Ruth Rose peered into the other tunnel. "I wonder how far it is to the beach," she said.

"It can't be that far," Dink said. "We're probably right under the castle."

"How are we gonna swim and carry these cages at the same time?" Josh asked. He glanced around the dark cave. "We need a raft or something."

"If the water's not too deep, we can walk out," Dink said.

He handed his cage to Ruth Rose, then stepped into the deeper water. It came up to his waist.

"It's kind of cold," he said, shivering, "but it's not very deep. We can carry the cages out."

"But what if it gets deeper?" Josh asked. "We can't carry the cages on our heads!"

"I have an idea," Ruth Rose said. "I read it in a Girl Scout magazine. It showed how to use your jeans as floats. You can make water wings by tying knots in the ankles and legs."

"You mean get undressed?" Josh said. "No way!"

"That's a great idea," Dink said. He climbed back out of the deep water, then kicked out of his sneakers and wet jeans. He tied knots in his jeans and put his sneakers back on.

Dink looked at Josh. "Come on," he said. "The water's getting deeper."

"Okay, but I feel weird," Josh muttered, pulling off his sneakers and jeans. The water reached just below his boxer shorts.

Dink tied knots in Josh's jeans, then dropped both pairs into the water. The air-filled jeans floated!

"Ready?" Dink said. They stepped into the water and balanced the two cages on top of the floating jeans.

"It works!" said Ruth Rose.

"This water's cold and yucky," Josh said.

"At least we can touch bottom," Dink said. "Okay, let's go."

The tunnel grew darker as they waded away from the cave. The water reached their chests, but got no higher.

The parrots were quiet, as if they knew they were being rescued.

"Do you think there are sharks in here?" Josh said. His voice echoed.

"No," Dink said. "Just a few man-eating lobsters."

Suddenly they heard a whispery sound in the darkness around them.

"What's that?" Ruth Rose asked.

"Calm down," Josh said, giggling. "It's just bats. We must've scared them."

"Are they friendly?" asked Ruth Rose.

"Not if you're an insect," Josh said.

Finally they saw daylight. Ahead was the ocean end of the tunnel.

"We did it, guys!" Dink said. They dragged the cages and soggy jeans to the beach near where they'd eaten their picnic.

"Boy, does the sun feel good!" Josh said, flopping down on the sand.

The kids rested and caught their

breath. Dink and Josh took the knots out of their jeans and spread them out to dry.

"I was thinking about these parrots," Josh said. "I have a book about endangered birds, and I think these guys are in it."

"Why would anyone hide endangered parrots in a cave?" Ruth Rose asked.

"Poachers," Josh said, pulling off his soaked sneakers. "Poachers catch rare animals and sell them for a lot of money."

"But who?"

Josh shrugged. "Someone who knows about the tunnel."

"I think I know who it is," Dink said.

Josh and Ruth Rose looked at him.

"Who?" Josh asked.

Dink looked sad. "Walker Wallace."

Chapter 11

"WHAT?" Ruth Rose yelled. "That's crazy!"

Dink shrugged. "I found one of the feathers in his Jeep and another on his boat."

Josh nodded slowly. "And when we had our picnic here yesterday, Wallis said Walker had been in the cave. Maybe he found the trapdoor in the playhouse."

"The footprints on the rug were big enough to be his," Dink said.

Ruth Rose stood up and wiped sand

off her wet jeans. "I don't believe you guys. Walker wouldn't break the law! And he sure wouldn't use his sister's house!"

"I hope not," Dink said. "Anyway, let's get the parrots up to the castle."

Dink and Josh tugged on their damp jeans and grabbed the cages. A few minutes later they burst into Wallis's kitchen.

She was writing at the table.

"We found out what's making those noises!" Dink blurted out.

The kids told Wallis about the tunnel to the cave and the parrots.

"A trapdoor in the playhouse!" Wallis exclaimed with wide eyes. "And a tunnel? How incredible!"

"It's like a secret passageway," Josh said. "Maybe pirates hid gold down there!"

"Well, I don't know about pirates,"

Wallis said. "But now I know how Emory Scott got all that marble and stuff up here!"

"What should we do with the parrots?" asked Ruth Rose.

"Show me," Wallis said.

They all trooped into the mud room. When the door opened, the parrots began flapping around in the cages. Their shrieks filled the room.

"Poor things," Wallis said. "Should we feed them? What do parrots eat?"

"Got any fruit?" Josh said. "That's what they'd eat in the rain forests."

Wallis went to the kitchen.

"I wonder where these guys came from," said Ruth Rose.

Josh studied the parrots. "Probably Africa or South America," he said.

"How would the poachers get them all the way to Maine?" Dink asked.

"By boat," Josh said. "Then a smaller

boat would bring them into the cave."

"A boat like Walk—"

Dink stopped talking as Wallis came back with two peeled bananas and a bunch of grapes. They dropped the fruit into the cages. The parrots grabbed the food in their beaks.

"They were starving!" Wallis said. She placed a bowl of water in each cage.

"I'm kind of hungry, too," Josh said. "We missed lunch."

"Well, we can't have that!" Wallis said. "Come into the kitchen."

While she made sandwiches, Dink explained about the light he'd seen in the woods the night before. "I bet there were more cages. They must take them out through the playhouse at night."

"We should hide down there and see who it is!" Ruth Rose said.

Wallis shook her head. "Absolutely

not. Those people could be dangerous!"

She brought out plates and napkins. "Today is Sunday, but tomorrow morning I'm going to call the state capitol. They must have someone who deals with poachers."

Wallis looked at the kids. "Promise me you'll stay out of that tunnel and cave."

Dink kicked Ruth Rose and Josh under the table.

"We promise," he said.

After lunch, the kids went back to the playhouse. They cleaned the dishes and swept the rug.

"I wish we could get these poacher guys," Dink said.

"I think we should sleep in the playhouse," Josh said. "Then if anyone comes, we'll grab them!"

"Josh, they'd grab *us* and stick us in

a cage," Ruth Rose said.

"Besides, Wallis would never let us stay down here," Dink said. "But I have another idea!"

At one-thirty in the morning, the kids were crouched by the window in Dink and Josh's dark room. They were fully dressed.

Josh yawned. "Maybe no one is coming tonight."

"Maybe they know we found the cages," Dink said. "Walker could've seen us from his boat."

"I still don't think it's Walker," Ruth Rose said. "But whoever it is will have to come to feed the parrots, right?"

"Right," Dink said. "Let's take turns watching. I'll go first. You guys can snooze."

"Wake me up if you see any bad guys!" Josh said, flopping on his bed.

"Well, I'm not tired," Ruth Rose said. "I hope they go to jail for a hundred years!"

She and Dink stared out into the darkness. The alarm clock counted away the minutes.

Josh began snoring.

"Look," Ruth Rose whispered a while later. "A firefly."

Dink saw a light moving slowly through the darkness. "Wake Josh," he told her. "That's no lightning bug!"

The kids tiptoed past Wallis's room, then hurried down the steps and out through the mud room door. Creeping silently, they approached the playhouse.

Moonlight fell on the clearing. A few yards from the playhouse, a dark car stood in the shadows.

Dink grabbed Josh and Ruth Rose and pointed. It was Walker's Jeep!

"I guess you were right," Ruth Rose whispered sadly.

The kids inched forward. Suddenly Dink saw a light coming from the play-house.

A man was bent over, pulling open the trapdoor! A glowing flashlight lay on the floor next to his feet.

The man stood up. In the flash-light's beam, Dink recognized who it was.

Ruth Rose grabbed his arm. "Ripley Pearce!" she whispered.

A moment later, Rip disappeared down the steps into the tunnel.

Suddenly Josh bolted around the corner of the playhouse and through the open door.

Before Dink could say anything, Josh slammed the trapdoor shut. Dink heard the spring lock snap into place.

Chapter 12

"What's Operation Game Thief?" Dink asked the next day.

"It's an 800 number you can call in Maine to report poachers," Wallis explained. She brought more hot pancakes to the table.

No one had gotten much sleep. After locking the trapdoor, Dink, Josh, and Ruth Rose had run back to wake up Wallis. She'd called 911 and reported poachers on her property.

The police had come and arrested Rip. The officers gave Wallis the Operation Game Thief phone number.

Wallis had then driven Walker's Jeep to his house and brought him back to the castle.

"The Maine Fish and Game Department will have plenty of questions for Rip," Walker said. "Trading in endangered animals is a federal crime."

"How did Rip get the parrots?" Josh asked.

"He must have contacts in the countries where they were captured," Walker said. "The police will be checking his phone bills to see whom he called."

"He probably used his own lobster boat," Wallis said, shaking her head. "No wonder it always looked so clean."

"Why did he have your Jeep?" Josh asked.

Walker speared another pancake. "Rip's car conked out a few days ago, so I let him borrow mine."

"It was a perfect set-up," Wallis said. "Rip needed money, and he had contacts who would pay a lot for rare parrots."

"I wonder if he sold any other animals," Josh said, "like monkeys or snakes."

"We may find out yet," Walker said. He winked at Josh. "What made you decide to shut the trapdoor on Rip?"

"I got mad!" Josh said. "I wanted him to see how it felt to be in a cage."

"So that green feather on Josh's sneaker came from Rip, right?" Dink asked.

Walker nodded. "He probably brought it into the Jeep on his foot. And the one you found on my boat got there the same way."

Josh blushed. "For a while we thought you were the poacher," he told Walker.

"Well, *I* never did!" Ruth Rose said.

Walker grinned at Ruth Rose. "Thanks! What made you so sure?"

"You're too busy," she answered. "And you wouldn't be mean to parrots. You threw those little crabs back in the water yesterday."

"What will happen to the parrots?" Dink asked.

"I assume they'll go back to where they came from," Walker said. "And Rip will most likely go to jail."

"And thanks to you kids, I won't have to hear any more strange noises," Wallis said.

She grinned shyly. "But to tell the truth, I think I'll miss the ghost of Emory Scott. I kind of liked living in a haunted castle!"

Just then a loud screech came from the mud room.

Collect clues with Dink, Josh, and Ruth Rose in their next exciting adventure,

THE EMPTY ENVELOPE!

Josh watched a dark blue car pull away from the library as he, Dink, and Ruth Rose came down the front steps.

"Hey," Josh said, "wasn't that car parked outside Ruth Rose's house?"

Ruth Rose shrugged. "I don't know."

They hurried up Woody Street.

Suddenly Josh grabbed Dink and Ruth Rose. He yanked them down behind Miss Alubicky's front hedge.

"What's wrong?" Dink asked.

"Now that blue car is in front of *your* house," Josh said.

The kids looked at each other.

"That can only mean one thing," Dink said. "Someone's following us!"